Bugs

Rose Inserra

Contents

What Are Bugs?

Bugs is the name for a special group of insects. It is one of the largest groups of insects in the world.

Some bugs live on land. They can live on the ground or on plants. Other bugs live in fresh water or seawater.

Bugs are the only kind of insects that can be found living on the surface of the ocean.

firebug

leafhopper

bedbug

pond skater

Like all insects, bugs have:

- two **antennae** (say: *an-ten-ee*)
- a head
- a thorax
- an abdomen
- six legs.

Most bugs have two sets of wings, **compound eyes** and tube-shaped mouthparts.

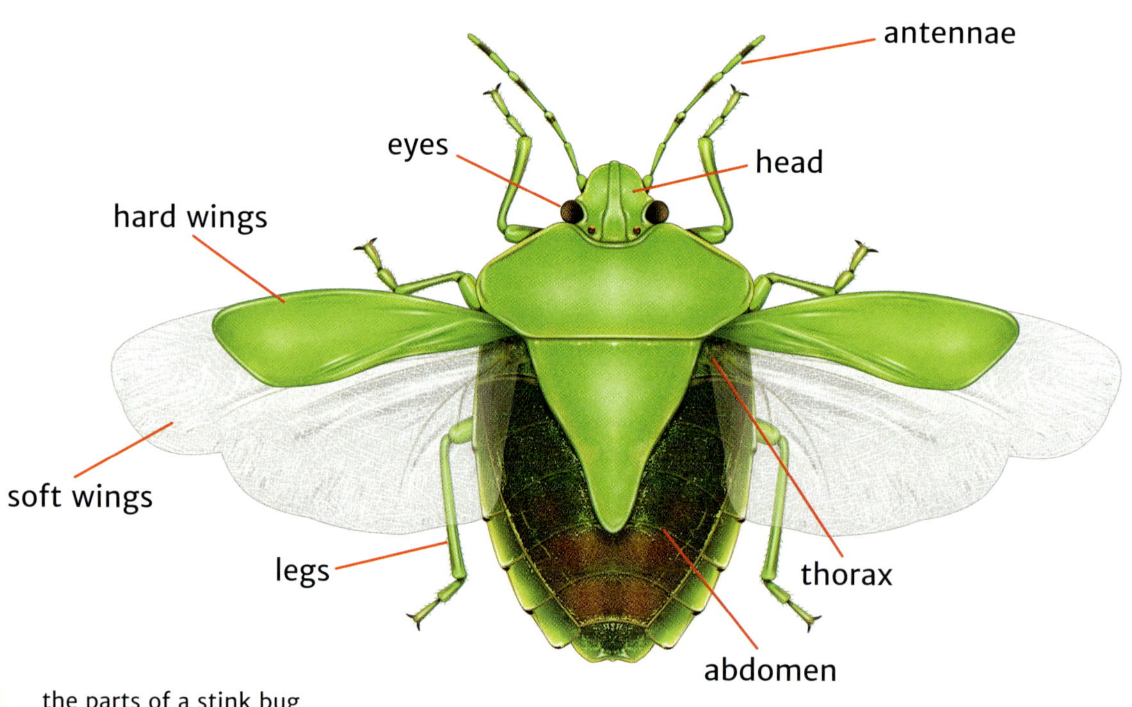

the parts of a stink bug

Bugs have a special way of eating.
They poke their tube-shaped mouthparts into their food and suck the juices out.

Most bugs feed on plants.
Others suck the blood of mammals and birds.
Some bugs feed on other insects.

The Life Cycle of a Bug

Bugs grow in a number of **stages**.
For many bugs, the first stage is laying eggs.
They lay their eggs in soil or on plants.
Some lay their eggs above or below the surface of water.

Young bugs, called nymphs, hatch from the eggs.
Nymphs look like adult bugs,
but they are smaller and do not have wings.

Nymphs moult, which means they lose their outer covering several times before they are fully grown.
The nymphs can grow bigger each time they moult.

All bugs are insects, but not all insects are bugs!

The Life Cycle of a Firebug

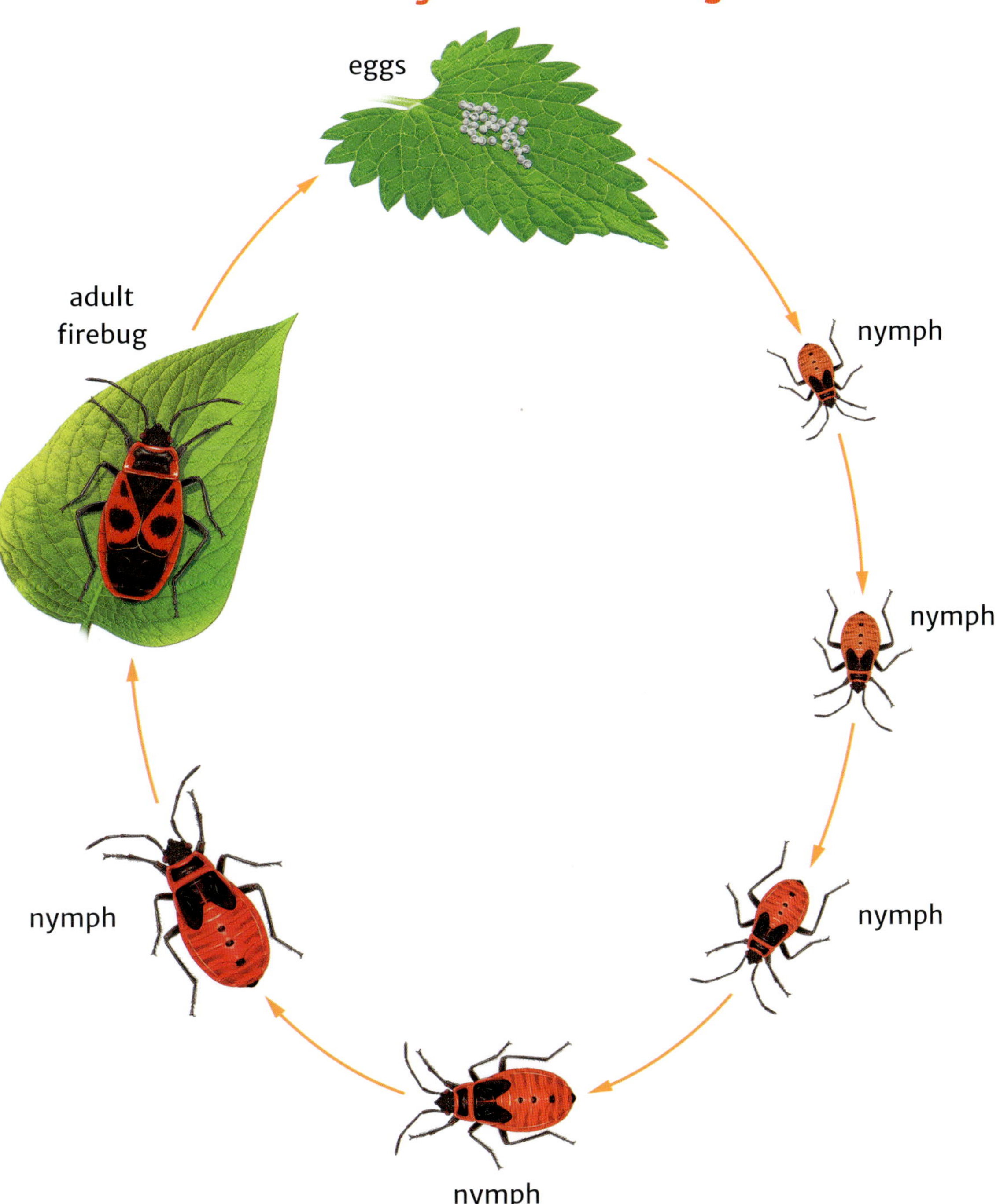

Different Kinds of Bugs

Leafhopper

Leafhoppers are bugs that are found on almost all kinds of plants.
They live in forests, deserts, grasslands, wetlands, fields and gardens.

Leafhoppers can move forwards, backwards and sideways, like a crab.
They leap easily from plant to plant.

This leafhopper is leaping to another plant.

Most leafhoppers are a few millimetres long, but some grow to 1.5 centimetres.

Leafhoppers can be hard to see because they are often **camouflaged** on the leaves and bark of trees.

This leafhopper is camouflaged on a leaf.

Leafhoppers are an important food for birds, lizards, spiders and insects like wasps.
Without leafhoppers for food, many of these creatures would not survive.

This leafhopper is being eaten by a spider.

Stink Bug

Stink bugs are found all around the world,
except in very cold places such as Antarctica.
These bugs let out a strong smell
when they feel **threatened**.
This usually smells like a herb called coriander,
but sometimes it is like rotten eggs.
That is why these bugs are called "stink" bugs.

Stink bugs live mostly on plants and trees. When it is cold, some types of stink bugs come inside houses to keep warm.

Once they are inside a house, they are very hard to get rid of!

This stink bug has come inside a house.

In houses and backyards, stink bugs find fruit like apples, berries and tomatoes to feed on. They suck the juice out of the fruit.

When stink bugs prick the skin of fruit, they leave some **saliva** inside it. This harms the fruit and then it is not good to eat.

Stink bugs are also called shield bugs.

Cicada

The cicada is a kind of bug that is found in all places around the world, except in Antarctica and the Arctic.

A female cicada lays its eggs in plant stems.
The eggs hatch into small, wingless nymphs.
The nymphs fall to the ground and burrow below the surface.

Cicada nymphs can live underground for many years.
They feed on the **sap** from plant roots.
They moult many times as they grow.

This cicada nymph is coming out from under the ground.

When the cicada nymph reaches its full size, it digs its way to the surface of the ground. Then it loses its outer covering for the last time. It is now an adult cicada.

There are about 3500 species of cicadas in the world.

Sometimes, cicadas can be heard singing.

Male cicadas make a sound using a special part of their bodies. They sing to **attract** a female. They can also make a sound so loud that it can help to keep predators away.

When many cicadas sing together, it makes a noisy song.

These cicadas are singing.

Pond Skater

Pond skaters are bugs that live on the surface of the water. These bugs are usually found in fresh water, like ponds and lakes, but some live on the ocean.

This view from above shows how pond skaters can walk on the water's surface.

Pond skaters have long, thin bodies and long legs.
They move about by walking, rowing and skating with their feet across the water.
Pond skaters can move quickly to catch prey or to get away from predators.

This pond skater is skating across the surface of the water.

Pond skaters feed on other insects.
They have hairs on their legs and feet,
which help them to catch their prey.
The hairs can feel any ripples on the water.
When the water moves, the pond skaters know that
another insect has fallen onto the surface of the water.

This view from above shows a pond skater catching a wasp on the water's surface.

Giant Water Bug

Giant water bugs live in fresh water, like lakes, ponds and **marshes**.
They are large bugs that grow up to 7 centimetres long.

Giant water bugs can breathe underwater.
They have a short tube that goes from their body up to the surface of the water, like a snorkel.

Giant water bugs prey on tadpoles, frogs, snails, small fish and other insects in the water.

This giant water bug has caught a fish to eat.

This giant water bug takes in air through its short tube.

Bugs are important insects.
They are food for many animals and birds.

Their tube-like mouthparts and special way of feeding make bugs an interesting group of insects to study.

green stink bug

brown stink bug

Glossary

antennae (*noun*) feelers or stalks on an insect's head

attract (*verb*) to get interest or attention

camouflaged (*adjective*) having colours or patterns that blend into a background

compound eyes (*noun*) eyes that are made up of different parts that work separately

marshes (*noun*) low, flat areas of land that are wet and muddy

saliva (*noun*) the liquid inside the mouth, also called spit

sap (*noun*) the sticky liquid inside trees and plants

stages (*noun*) the separate parts of a process

threatened (*adjective*) in danger

Index